Jacob

Book 4

COPYRIGHT

© Lynn Donovan 2020

Cover Copyright © 2020 Virginia McKevitt

This is a work of fiction. All characters and events portrayed in this novel are fictitious and are products of the author's imagination. Any resemblance to actual events, locales, or persons, living or dead, is entirely coincidental.

ISBN: 9798667173557

CONTENTS

ACKNOWLEDGMENTS

Thank you to everybody in my life who has contributed in one way or another to the writing of this book. My husband, my children, my children-in-law, and my grandchildren. You all are my unconditional fans. My BETA reader and grammar guru who make me look gooder than I am. [Bad grammar intended.] My fellow author friends who chat with me daily to exchange ideas, encourage, maintain sanity, and keep me from being a total recluse/hermit.

Mostly I thank God for the talent he has given me. I hope to hear you say, "Well done, my good and faithful servant," when I cross the Jordan and run into your arms —Many, many years from now. :).

ABOUT THIS SERIES

Sons of Honor Series
>Adam
>Seth
>Jonah
>Jacob
>Reuben
>Benjamin

Prologue

Lantern, Texas - 1867

Ten-year-old Jacob Featherstone pushed his favorite girl, Charlene Chance, in the tree swing at his Great Uncle Harrison's home. It was the second annual Founder's Day Dinner and Fourth of July celebration for Lantern, his hometown. It was stupid to call it that. July 4th was days away! Something like four days. It wasn't 'til Thursday, in fact. That was forever from now, and they weren't having a week-long rodeo contest like last year, to fill the gap between Sunday and Thursday.

His momma and Charlene's momma had new husbands. So did a whole lot of women whose husbands had died in the War. So Jacob reckoned there was no need to put on another rodeo. Although last year was a lot of fun. He supposed the five-hundred-dollar prize was too much for Lantern to have a rodeo like that every year, or ever again.

Both he and Charlene had been warned by their momma's to not get dirty. They wore their Sunday best clothes since it was Sunday and they had just left church. Charlene's mom, Charity Brunston, had wagged her finger at the two of them when they ran off from the grownups to play. How stupid to expect kids to stay clean just because they wore their church clothes.

Jacob could have run home and changed, but Charlene lived way out of town at Second Chance Ranch. She couldn't go home to change and come back, she'd miss the whole Founder's Day fun and food. It was one of the few times all the cousins and other relations came together in one place for the whole day.

Uncle Harrison had nice big trees, perfect for tree swings and climbing. He had hung two of them on either side of the cottonwood. His house had been in Lantern the longest since he was one of the original founders.

It was a subject they studied in school, "Lantern, Texas, Our Founding Fathers." There wasn't a textbook or anything. Mrs. Janson just knew all about it and wrote stuff on the board. The students were expected to write papers about their favorite detail.

Jacob didn't see what the big deal was. Anybody who lived here all their lives, like him and his brothers, knew about Uncle Harrison Lantern and his brothers. Aunt Gloria and Uncle Harrison were married out east before they came to Texas to settle a place. Shoot, everyone in Lantern was family, cousins at least. Even Charlene was Jacob's second cousin. Nobody could help but know who the founders were and how they were all related. Uncle Harrison was the pastor, too. He talked about that stuff every Sunday.

"Charlene?" Jacob pushed her as the seat swung back to his reach. "How's it going with your new dad?"

"I *told* you *not* to call me *Charlene*!" She spoke over her shoulder and stretched out her legs to make herself go higher.

Abigail Drucker ran by, chasing Jacob's baby brother, Benjamin. She overheard Charlene reprimand Jacob and hollered. "Charlene, Charlene, Charlene!"

Jacob watched them run past, cringing over what he'd said, and then Abigail made it worse by chanting her given name.

"Sorry, Charley. So, how's it going?"

"Fine, I s'pose. How about you?"

"Yeah, we like Mister O'Mallory. We call him Poppa Monty. What do you call Hezekiah?"

"I just call him Daddy." She sounded sad.

"It's hard, isn't it?"

"Yeah. But Mom likes it when I call him Daddy. She don't cry no more, so I reckon he's all right."

"Charley?" Jacob glanced at his twin brother, Jonah, on the other side of the tree, pushing Theodora Farmington. "When we grow up, you wanna get married?"

She laughed. "Jacob Featherstone! I can't marry you! You're a whole year younger than me. Besides, how do you know when you grow up you'll still like me?"

"Oh, I know." Jacob assured her. "I know exactly what I want when I grow up."

She swung away from him, stretching out long as her boots rose high in the air. Her hair hung down nearly touching the grass, then she sat up as her swing came back toward him. "Oh, do you? And what is that?"

"I'm gonna be a doctor, like my real dad, and Momma. I'm gonna marry you, and we will have four children. A boy, and a girl, and twins like me and Jonah."

"Really?" She put her feet down, abruptly stopping the swing. It fell from her skirt as she stood and turned at the waist to look at him. "You're that certain how everything will be?"

Jacob crossed his hands in front of his hips. He felt exposed, vulnerable under her scrutiny. "Yes."

"Well, we better seal it with a kiss." She stepped away from the swing and walked toward him. "My mom says if I kiss a boy, I'll be committed to him for life. So we better seal this so it has to come true."

He waited for her to get close enough and then he closed his eyes. She kissed him, right on the lips! His heart pounded so hard in his chest he thought he might pass out. He opened his eyes to find her just inches from his face, grinning like a 'possum eating cactus. He smiled. "So, it's sealed."

"I reckon so, it's sealed now and forever, Jacob Featherstone. Someday I will marry you."

Abigail Drucker ran up to them and halted just behind Jacob. "Ummmm, I'm tellin'." She ran off. Charley and Jacob watched her run away. They turned to each other and laughed.

Chapter One

Founder's Day, Lantern, Texas 1881

Jacob pushed his gal, Charley Chance, in the swing at Uncle Harrison's homestead, just like he did when they were kids. There were three swings hanging now from the huge cottonwood tree where there had been only two. The Lantern family grew bigger, and newcomers caused the town to grow even larger. Founder's Day Dinner had become a huge affair. Jacob almost felt guilty for taking up the swing when there were so many young children running around. But he had his reasons.

"Remember when you kissed me, right here at this swing, and we promised someday we'd get married?"

She straightened her limbs, making the swing go higher than what he pushed. It wasn't until the swing came back and he pushed her again that she answered him. "Yeah, but we were… what? Ten or eleven then? You said you wanted to be a doctor, and we'd get married, and have four children." She paused. "A boy and a girl, and twins like you and Jonah." She laughed. "But, Jacob, I didn't realize then that you becoming a doctor meant you'd want me to leave Lantern."

"It's just four or five years, Charlene."

"Do. Not. Call. Me. Charlene!"

"I'm sorry. Your mother calls you Charlene. I would think now that you are twenty-five you'd drop your childhood nickname."

"It's not just a nickname. *Charley* is who I am. *Charlene* is who everybody else wants me to be."

He pushed her again and considered what she meant.

Finally, he spoke again. "I guess, when we were little, I thought I could just study with Momma and be a doctor. That's a lot like how she became the town doctor. But nowadays a person can't just read everything he can get his hands on and start practicing medicine, like I've done. Ya gotta actually go to a university and earn a degree. Only… that's real expensive."

"Times have changed. For the better, I s'pose." She put her feet down and stepped out of the swing. "I don't want to stop you from achieving your life's dreams, Jacob. Go! Go to university, get a degree in medicine. Be a doctor!"

"But—" he held the rope attached to the swing

seat. "I want you with me, as my wife."

"I-I can't leave Mother. She's not well. Hezekiah, I mean Daddy, is great with her, but… she needs me."

Jacob hung his head. "But— I love you, and… we sealed it with a kiss."

"We were children!" She walked away from him. He stared at her with the rope still in his hand.

"I'll go with you to Boston, Jacob." Abigail Drucker slipped up behind him. "I ain't got nothing holding me back here in Lantern." He turned to glare at her, but his eyes ran down her womanly, shapely figure. His throat suddenly went drier than the Odessa Dessert. "Th-thank you Abigail. I appreciate it, but—"

She twirled a lock of hair around her finger. "I know… you're in love with that Charlene Chance. You've always been sweet on her. Too bad she's not sweet on you." Abigail stepped up closer to Jacob, and leaned in to his ear. "I could be sweet on you."

Her perfume lingered with Jacob when Abigail leaned back from him. Words failed him. He just stared at her. She giggled, a tinkling, sweet sound, and scurried off.

"Can I swing, now?" A young girl demanded.

Jacob glanced down at her. "Oh. Sure. Sorry."

He took a step to go catch up with Charley—

A gunshot echoed from town. Some women screamed in alarm. Jacob stiffened. Something's happening in town. He scanned the people for his mother. He knew she'd be going in case someone was hurt. Of course someone was hurt! A gun just went off! He rushed through the people.

Sheriff Patience barked orders. "Everybody stay here! Do NOT leave this place."

Jacob spotted his mother and her nurse, Evelyn Graham, mounting horses. Adam mounted too. Jacob wanted to go, but should he? Momma always said too many people at an accident did more harm than good. He thought about who all he saw leaving. "One, two, three, four, five." Five people were already a lot. He'd better stay back. If Momma needed him, she'd send for him. And he'd be ready.

A gun fired in town. Charley stumbled. Where's Mom? Her eyes roved over the crowd. Everybody ran toward the edge of the two-acre property as if they could see what was going on in town, while Charley ran the opposite direction. She moved toward Uncle Harrison and Aunt Gloria's house. Mom was probably inside. The sun bothered her too much to stay out in it for too long. She said it drained her.

Charley had no idea what was wrong with her mother but whatever it was, she grew weaker. Charley had to cook and help her mother dress and bathe, and other private things a woman did on a daily basis. Daddy, as her husband of the last fourteen years, was perfectly willing to help, but Mom preferred a woman's presence, and Charley was the only woman on the ranch.

There was no way she could go off with Jacob Featherstone for four or five years. In fact, if she and Jacob *did* get married, Charley would insist they live at Second Chance Ranch, so she could continue to help her mom. She had never mentioned all this to Jacob because she knew how much he wanted to be a doctor.

He asked Cousins Faith and Purity at the library, to get textbooks about medical practices and had read every single one of them. If one could read themselves into being a doctor, Jacob certainly had done enough to make that happen. But his momma had assured him that he needed to go to a university to get the degree and title. The family wasn't hurting for money, but going to a university was expensive. And if she and Jacob were married, he'd have that responsibility added on to trying to attend classes. She shook her head. There was no way she could see any of that working out.

How could she stand in his path of fulfilling this one dream he'd had since— she couldn't remember a time he didn't talk about becoming a doctor. Of course, he'd talked about them getting married for just as long, but one excluded the other in her mind. Her mom needed her here. And he needed to go away in order to become a doctor.

"Mom!" She found her in the kitchen, sitting at the breakfast table. Those who were in the house had gathered with a pot of tea and were visiting over lady-finger sandwiches. The loud sound of the gun going off was muffled inside and had not alarmed these ladies. "Are you all right?"

"Yes, Charlene, dear. Why do you ask?"

"Well…" Charley swallowed. Should she worry her mother? "Something has happened in town, and Sheriff Patience and Doctor Honor have gone to see what it is. I just wanted to be sure if you heard about it, you were not… upset."

"Upset?" Charity looked at her companions.

Hope Monroe and Faith Burke frowned. "What happened in town, Charlene."

Charley cringed but didn't correct them. "I-I don't know yet. It sounded like a gunshot."

"A gun!" Charley's mom exclaimed. "We heard a loud pop, but thought someone had gotten into the fireworks. Oh, dear me. Do you suppose…" Her eyes darted to Hope, then Faith. "You don't suppose it's some of those bushwackers, again?"

They shrugged. Hope stood. "Let's go see if anybody has come back to tell us what's happening."

"Yes, let's go to the veranda." Charity said with a heavy sigh. She stood slowly and reached out for Charley to help her walk. Charley rushed to her mother and took her arm to escort her to a chair on the wide, wrap-around porch.

Chapter Two

Jacob stood with his twin and two younger brothers, watching for someone to come back from town to let everyone at the Founder's Day Celebration know what was going on. The huge dinner had been forgotten. Normally people would be serving plates from the three open spits of cooked meat and long tables with assorted side dishes brought by all the people. The food was being ignored for news from town.

His patience was wearing thin. Their older brother, Seth, had volunteered to stay with Sheriff Caleb in town while the celebration moved to Uncle Harrison's. Could it be that he was the one who fired a gun? Jacob clenched his jaw. Or was Seth the one

—

"I can't stand this, I'm going to find out what happened." Jacob said to no one in particular.

Benjamin, Jacob's youngest brother, grabbed Jacob's arm. "But… no, you can't. Sheriff Patience told everybody stay here."

Jacob sighed. "If Momma needs help… I could help."

"Miss Graham went with her!"

"Ben! I'm going."

Jacob's twin, Jonah, turned to him. "I'll come with you."

"No. I'll go find out what happened and come back to let y'all… and everybody know."

Jonah sighed. "Probably better to limit the number of people in town."

"Yeah." Jacob nodded. "My thoughts, exactly."

Benjamin sighed. "All right. But please be careful. Don't you get hurt, too!"

Jacob glared at him. "I won't get in the way." He considered Benjamin. "And tell Charley where I've gone and that I'll be back with news."

Benjamin looked toward the house. "I'll let her know."

Jacob eased his heals into Doc Holliday's sides. The horse leapt into a gallop.

"You be careful, Jacob Featherstone!" Abigail Drucker yelled from somewhere behind him.

The Lantern National Bank's door stood open as Jacob rode down Main Street. He looked away from the door and obvious blood on the floor to see Poppa Monty and Momma carrying a stretcher toward the clinic. Jacob rode up alongside them. Evelyn Graham trailed behind, holding a bloody cloth in her hands and looked like she'd been crying. Where was Sheriff Caleb? Or Seth? Who was on the cot? Jacob hurried his horse ahead and leapt off at the clinic's entrance, looped his horse's rein to the post, and waited for them to get close enough to ask. "Who —?"

"It's Seth." Poppa Monty blurted. "Gunshot to the back."

"What? Who sh—"

"Bushwackers!" Momma answered. "Caleb rode out after them."

Jacob nodded. "You need anything?"

"We've got this handled, son." Momma looked at him sternly and turned her focus on getting the stretcher inside the clinic.

Jacob stayed on the boardwalk, watching them enter the facility. "Is-" he swallowed. "Is he all right?"

Miss Graham turned back to Jacob before she closed the door with him on the outside. "We honestly don't know."

Jacob stared at the closed door. What was he supposed to tell everybody back at the dinner? He turned to his horse. "What should I do, Doc Holliday?"

His horse lifted his head and whinnied. Did he have any idea how serious the situation was right now? Or the weight of the responsibility of being the only person who was available to ride back and let everyone know his brother had been shot? "Come on. We've gotta let them know something."

Jacob mounted Doc Holliday and kicked him into a run. He didn't want to scare the people, but there was no way to make the news sound like good tidings. All he could do was tell what he knew, not speculate about anything he didn't. And not mention the bloody cloth Miss Graham was carrying. Jacob's stomach clenched tight. He swallowed and lifted his chin. He could do this. He'd seen Momma deliver bad news hundreds of time. He'd do like she did.

The people rushed to him as he dismounted at Uncle Harrison's. "Adam was just here!" "He took Purity back to town." "Is Seth dead?" "What's going on?" "I heard it was bushwackers." "Is it true the bank got robbed?"

Jacob swallowed hard as he walked through the pressing crowd. "Let me get where everybody can hear." He begged them, as he walked toward the veranda.

"Folks." He raised his hands to quiet everyone. "All I know is there *was* an *attempt* to rob the bank… and my brother…" He swallowed. "My brother, Seth, got shot, but he's still alive. Momma's with him at the clinic and…" He searched the faces for Charley, wishing she was standing beside him. He needed her strength. "That… that's all I know."

A hand gently touched his shoulder and he turned to see Charley. He almost threw his arms around her, but he remembered one more thing he needed to say. "Oh, yes, it *was* bushwackers, but Sheriff Caleb has gone after them."

A chatter rose among the people listening. They moved away from the veranda and headed to whatever means they had used to get up the hill. Horses, wagons, buggies, or walking; people moved away from Uncle Harrison's house and toward the clinic downtown.

Jacob put his arm around Charley, she turned into his embrace. "I'm so sorry," she muttered against his shoulder. With all the people moving away from the veranda, he felt less public and let go of his pent up emotions, letting tears slip out against her hair. "Oh, Charley. There was so much blood. I just don't see how Seth's gonna be all right."

She shook him slightly. "Now, don't think that way. Your mom is amazing and if anybody can fix this, it's her."

Jacob lifted his head, wiping his eyes. "You're right. I honestly don't know how bad his injuries are. All I saw was a body on a stretcher and Miss Graham carrying a blood-soaked cloth. Momma always says it looks worse than it is."

"There you go." Charley assured him. "Looks like everyone's heading to town, you s'pose we ought to go, too?"

Jacob looked deeply into her eyes. "I-I want to be there, at the clinic, to know the minute Momma says how he's doing, but that clinic ain't all that big."

Charley nodded. "I understand. Look, I'll get Mom and go home. You can let us know when you can."

Jacob squeezed her hands. "Thank you. I will. Soon as I can."

Jacob joined his brothers and they rode into town, pushed through the crowd and into the clinic. Purity, Adam, and Poppa Monty sat in the waiting area. Anxiety and worry written all over their faces.

Jacob, his twin, Reuben, and Benjamin sat down to wait.

Gunshot wound. Jacob ran through his memory of medical books he had read. *Shot in the back.* Could be internal organ damage, liver, bowels, kidneys. It all depended on where Seth got shot. Must *not* have been high, that would have been heart or lungs. Seth would have been less likely to have lived. It had to be low.

Jacob wasn't sure, but with the manner in which Momma was acting, Jacob sensed she was concerned about Seth's lower back. Jacob stood and paced the clinic's parlor. No one chastised him for doing it. Everyone worried in their own way. He looked at his family. Did any of them want to go back there where Momma was working on Seth as badly as he did and look in on the surgery? He glanced down the hall. An urgency swelled in his heart. He wanted to learn how to do what Momma did. He wanted to be back there, assisting her, or performing the surgery himself.

He had to find a way to go to university! And if he was going to go to university, he might as well go to the one that had the best medical training. As far as he knew, that was Harvard Medical College in Boston, Massachusetts.

But Charley! How could he convince Charley to go with him? Her momma looked pale, she was tired, weak. Could it be something to do with her blood? What had Momma diagnosed Charity with? Anemia caused those symptoms, but this seemed different. Jacob sat down. If he could help Charity, maybe Charley would be willing to go to Boston with him. Then he could get a medical degree and come back to Lantern and take over Momma's practice. Or at least help her with her practice. He smiled. Momma said she wanted him to take her place, but did she really? She loved what she did, and she was good at it.

Evelyn Graham walked toward them in the parlor. Her apron was covered in blood. Jacob swallowed. She looked tired and worried. What would she say? Was Seth dead? Jacob's gut tightened as he waited for her to speak.

"Well, he's alive."

Jacob blew out relief. Thank God! Miss Graham continued telling about the bullet being close to Seth's spine, but Jacob's attention went to his

Momma as she walked down the hall toward them. She, too, looked exhausted, but pleased. Purity cried and Momma sat beside her answering questions and generally comforting her. Jacob wanted to squat at his Momma's knees to listen to every word, but held himself back.

Bullet close to spine— paralysis. Seth might be paralyzed. But Momma wasn't sure. It was a matter of time. It was a matter of how close and how much damage was caused by the bullet and her retrieving it from his body. Taking a bullet out of the body could be just as harmful as when it was shot into the body.

Jacob watched Momma's eyes trying to determine how she felt about the surgery results. Confident. Jacob sensed she was confident she had done what she could. Perhaps Seth has a good chance of recovering and walking again.

"I want you all to go home."

Jacob snapped his attention with Momma's words. She felt Seth was fine for now, otherwise she'd suggest they stay. That gave Jacob more relief in his heart than anything else. Momma continued and Jacob almost chanted her final words, because she said them so often "God only knows at this point."

Yeah, she was feeling good about his recovery, but she knew the final word was up to the man upstairs. Jacob and she had many conversations about this very subject.

Purity, of course, insisted on staying with Seth. Everybody expected that. Jacob smirked. Momma agreed, no surprise there either. "…the rest of you, go home!"

"Yes ma'am." Jacob chuckled.

"I'll get word to you as soon as we know something."

Jacob glanced at his brothers. They looked uncertain about leaving, but Jacob knew exactly what he was going to do. He nodded to assure them it was alright to leave and he walked out, leapt on Doc Holliday, and headed straight to where he could get some answers.

Chapter Three

Jacob should ride out to Second Chance Ranch, but he wanted to check on something first. He went inside the little library and rifled through the information on Harvard Medical College. Seth's recovery was contingent with healing and healing was contingent on maintaining his strength. Even if there was some damage to his spine, there had to be —

Jacob looked through a list of courses and the textbooks required by the professors. He found what he had in mind and wrote everything down so he could ask Purity or Faith to order the book. As he flipped the pages to close the catalog, he spied something interesting. He pulled another piece of paper and wrote the information down.

Pleased with what he had found, he tucked the notes into his breast pocket and rode out to see Charley.

Dusk dimmed the horizon as he knocked on the ranch house door and waited. Silence radiated through the house. Where were they? Charity's buggy sat by the barn, her horse had been unharnessed and probably taken in to be brushed down and fed. Andre Hernandez was old, but he took good care of Charity's livestock. Jacob turned from the door and strode to the barn. As expected, Señor Hernandez had put the buggy horse in her stall.

"*Hola*." Jacob greeted him. "I tried the house. Do you know where Charley might be?"

Hernandez had tack slung over his shoulder. He looked concerned. "*Señora* Brunston, no look so good. *Señorita* Charley take her upstair right away."

"I'm sorry to hear that." Jacob looked back at the house. "I suppose Charley's busy helping her momma."

"*Sí*. She no look good." Hernandez shook his head.

"So, how are you, Señor Hernandez? You still cattin' around?" Jacob laughed.

Hernandez smiled wickedly. "No. Those young *vaqueros* asked me to give them some room." He laughed from his belly. "So, I stay on ranch and let them have their chance with the pretty *señoritas*." He made a guttural laugh that sounded mischievous and made Jacob laugh, too.

"That's mighty kind of you *Señor* Hernandez."

"Yeah… I gotta give them *hombres* a chance." He waddled toward the tack room and hung up what he had taken off Charley's horse. "You go on in. *Señorita* Charley no mind you coming in. Just don't go upstair without letting her know you come."

Jacob smiled. "All right, and if I get in trouble, I'll tell her you told me to go in."

Hernandez laughed. Jacob laughed with him and walked to the house. He knocked again, just for good measure, then tried the door. It was not locked. Slowly he entered the house. He'd come here all his life with Momma. She and Charity were first cousins and as close as sisters. He'd been in love with Charley ever since he realized she was a girl and what that meant to a boy. As far as he was concerned, they'd been betrothed since they kissed on Founder's Day when he was ten.

"Charley!" He called out, alerting her that he was in the house. "It's me, Jacob!"

"Jacob?" Charley's voice sounded scared. "Could you come here?"

"Sure." He took the stairs two at a time. "I'm here. What's wrong?"

Charity sat in a chaise lounge, her head back, one hand on her chest. She gasped for air. Her eyes were wide with fear, so we're Charley's. "What's wrong?"

"I don't know. I helped her upstairs and she collapsed here." Charley rushed to him. "She says she can't breathe, Jacob. What do I do?"

Jacob nodded and walked up to Charity. He squatted beside her and took her hands into his. Speaking as calmly as possible. "Cousin Charity, it's Jacob Featherstone. Look at me."

Her eyelids fluttered and darted about the room, landing on Jacob. "Oh…, Jacob… I… can't… draw… a… breath."

"Charity, look at me. Breathe with me."

He breathed slowly and steadily. She followed his lead and soon she was breathing much better. He continued breathing with her, nodding to assure her she was all right. Out of the corner of his eye he saw Charley standing back with her hands crisscrossed over her heart.

This had frightened her. He wanted to find out what was causing Charity to be like this. Once the situation with Seth settled down, Jacob committed to discussing Charity's symptoms with his mother. There had to be something they could do to help her. If Momma didn't know, maybe he could find out for himself.

"Thank you for helping Mom." Charley walked Jacob to the front door.

"I wish I could do more. How long has she been having these… spells?"

"She gets tired easily, and when she does, she has trouble breathing. She clutches her chest like her heart hurts." Charley shook her head. "It's why I can't leave her, Jacob."

"I understand. Really, I do. But surely there's something… I'll keep looking for a way to help her."

"Thank you." Charley kissed Jacob on the cheek. "You're going to make a great doctor. You care so much for people.

Jacob pressed his lips into a thin line. Guilt swamped his face. "Charley, to be honest with you, I want to help your mom for very selfish reasons. I feel terrible telling you that. But it's true. It's not compassion for a patient that drives me to find a cure for Charity." He hung his head. "I'll keep searching."

Charley held his elbow as they walked out to the barn. Andre had watered Doc Holliday and had him ready for Jacob. "Thank you, *Señor* Hernandez."

"*De nada.*" Hernandez dipped his head. "Please let us know how *Señor* Seth is doing, *sí*?"

"Of course." Jacob mounted Doc Holliday. He turned to Charley and smiled. She returned his smile as he reined his horse and left the ranch. The moon lit his way down the road.

Charley dropped the smile and her shoulders and walked back into the house. She collapsed on the divan. She'd give anything to marry Jacob Featherstone tomorrow and ride off with him to Boston, or anywhere he wanted to go. She could work while he went to university. She had skills. She helped Hezekiah with the accounts, or she could teach the little ones to read and write, or cook at a diner. And she'd do it willingly for Jacob, just until he got his degree. Then, she'd be willing to move back here, or wherever he wanted to live. She didn't care. As long as she could be his wife, raise his children, and grow old at his side.

It had been her dream ever since she kissed him when she was eleven. She and Jacob Featherstone were sealed in fate to be married. But life changed and Mom grew sick as Charley grew up. Charley was well past the age of spinster now. She reckoned this was how her life would be— alone at Second

Chance Ranch 'til she died an old maid.

What choice had she had, really? She couldn't possibly give her heart to anyone other than Jacob, and he wanted to become a doctor. If she were to give in to his proposal, she'd only tie him down to Lantern and he'd never get the schooling he needed. How could she do that to him? He'd probably grow bitter toward her for being the obstacle that kept him from going to Harvard.

She couldn't bear the thought of Jacob ever having any feelings for her other than love and affection. Her heart would break into tiny pieces if he were ever bitter toward her. She loved him too much to keep him from achieving his goals, even if that meant she had to watch Abigail Drucker take her place at Jacob's side.

A shiver rippled down Charley's spine. Oooo, that Abigail! She'd leap on that wagon with Jacob in a heartbeat, if she could. To be honest, why Jacob hadn't accepted her advances was beyond Charley's understanding. That girl had grown into a beautiful woman. Any man would be pleased as pie to have her in his marriage bed. She had followed the Featherstone boys around like a lost puppy most of her life. Jacob had oftentimes been the one she flitted to most. Why none of them ended up with her was a mystery.

Charley stood. *Well, I better get some sleep while I can.*

Chapter Four

Jacob rode home hoping to find Momma there. It would mean Seth was all right and give Jacob a moment to discuss Charity Chance's condition with her. All the lamps were out but one in the kitchen window, facing the carriage house where he would see it when he put Doc Holliday up for the night. Everything he wanted to do would have to wait until tomorrow. He climbed the stairs and went to bed.

The next morning Poppa Monty wrestled with a hind quarter of beef to bring it up from the root cellar. He'd brought it home from the Founder's Day Dinner. Jonah waited in the kitchen to help section the beef into manageable size meals, Reuben and Benjamin were gathering eggs and milking the cow.

Jacob wished he had that textbook he had found in the Harvard catalog. He'd love to stay upstairs and peruse the information. The sooner he could get the information to Seth, the sooner his older brother would get to healing. "Healing in motion," the book called it. Soon as Momma let Seth go home, Jacob would ask Purity to order the textbook for the library.

A loud knock, or rather a pounding, rapped on

the front door.

"I'll get it!" Jacob hollered to Poppa Monty and Jonah.

"All right, son." Monty replied.

Jacob opened the door and cocked his head back. "Oh, Abigail. What brings you out this early?" She was dressed to the nines in her Sunday best and loaded down with dishes.

"I brought your side dishes. Y'all left your food at the Founder's Day Dinner… well, I guess we can't call it a dinner. No one ate a bite. Everybody gathered their dishes and took 'em home, except y'all." She gasped as if she'd said something rude. "Of course we all understand why, Seth being shot and all."

Jacob frowned. "That was thoughtful, I s'pose. Uh, thank you."

"Of course. I'm happy to be of help." She stepped forward even though Jacob had not invited her in. Her hands were encumbered with carefully stacked bowls and a baking dish. He looked at the dishes, wondering how he could take them from her and not cause her to drop the carefully stacked collection. She paused when he didn't move out of her way. "Momma stored these down in the cellar overnight so everything would keep."

"Well, we appreciate her for that." Jacob decided there was no way for him to prevent her from walking in. "Come in, please, uh, put them in the kitchen." He led the way. "We appreciate you bringing them."

"Anything I can do to help the Featherstones." She looked around the kitchen, deciding what to do with her load. Jacob rushed to her and took the top dish, set it down on the breakfast table, took the next dish and continued to relieve her of her burden until she was free to set the last two down. "Thank you, Jacob." She smiled and batted her eyelashes.

Poppa Monty smiled graciously. "Thank you, Abigail. That was very kind of you. Now we have something to go with this hind quarter." He chuckled.

"Oh, how sweet. I'd love to stay after church and eat with you."

Poppa Monty darted confused eyes to Jacob who lifted his eyebrows in reply. Monty stammered, "You-you want to walk to church with us?"

She latched onto Jacob's elbow. "I declare, you Featherstones are the nicest people."

Jacob glared at his twin, who was smirking

behind Poppa Monty. "Uh, Jonah, don't you want to escort Miss Abigail to church?"

"No, you look like you've got this under control."

"But I—" Jacob looked at Abigail, who instantly smiled sweetly and squeezed his arm all the more tightly. "I reckon your folks will be in the service?"

"Oh, I'm certain they will. Momma wouldn't let Papa shy away from church, ever."

Jacob swallowed. He couldn't think of a way to get away from Abigail without being utterly rude, but he feared what Charley would think when she saw him walking with Abigail. This wasn't going to be easy. Surely Abigail would leave his side and go sit with her parents once they got inside the church. If not, Jacob worked out that he could move to the pews where Charley's family sat.

"So." Poppa Monty said with a grin. "We ready for church?"

The boys filed out the back door. Poppa Monty held out his arm for Jacob and Abigail to go ahead of him and closed the door behind them. They piled into the wagon. Jacob helped Abigail onto the bench beside Poppa Monty and then climbed into the wagon bed. "Oh, Jacob, please sit with me." Abigail whined as she patted the bench to her right.

Jacob looked at her, then glanced at his brothers. Jonah suppressed his mirth. Reuben and Benjamin refused to look at Jacob. "Uh, sure."

Jacob climbed over and sat beside her.

She clung to his elbow all the way up the hill as if she might fall off the bench. He couldn't see any way she could fall, considering she was snuggly tucked between him and Poppa Monty. But there was no way he could get out of her grasp without making a big production out of pulling away from her. Jacob closed his eyes and prayed Charley and her family were late to church.

Jacob helped Abigail down and instantly was back in her clutches. His elbow ached from her tight grip. He walked her into church, looking around for the Druckers, so she could go sit with them. But he didn't see them. With a sigh, he walked to where the Featherstones always sat and slide into the pew with Abigail still on his elbow.

His momma entered and came to sit with Poppa Monty. Jacob smiled. Her being here meant good news. Nearly everybody flocked to Momma to ask about Seth. Jacob used the distraction to turn and look for Charley. Spotting her, he turned to Abigail.

"Excuse me a moment."

He rushed to Charley. "Hey."

She glared at him. "So, I see you're sitting with Abigail Drucker this morning."

Jacob rolled his eyes. "More like she's sitting with us. She brought our dishes from Founder's Day over this morning and I haven't been able to figure out how to get away from her since."

Charley laughed. "Sounds like an interesting problem." She turned to see that her dad assisted her mother down the aisle and that she was all right. They slid into the pew where they normally sat. "Well, enjoy your company for church." A mischievous grin quivered at the corner of her mouth, yet he detected sadness in her eyes.

Jacob sighed. "But—" he watched her slide into the pew behind them and sit without another word. "Charley?"

She glanced up at him. But Uncle Harrison began to speak and Aunt Gloria began playing the piano softly while he spoke. He asked Momma how Seth was doing.

Jacob needed to sit down, somewhere. He returned to his family and slid into the pew. Abigail quickly scooted to make room beside her. He only had two choices: to sit beside her or make a spectacle of himself. He sat with a heavy sigh and tried to focus on Uncle Harrison.

After church let out, the Druckers collected their daughter. She pouted over her shoulder as they gathered her and walked down the hill for their home. At last, Jacob was free to speak to Mercy Coffey. Mercy and Adam were surrounded by people asking about Seth. Jacob slid up beside her. "Mercy, could I speak to you a minute?"

Mercy stepped away from Adam. "Of course."

"I'm concerned about Cousin Charity. She seems so exhausted all the time. I'm going to talk to Momma when things settle down, but I was wondering if you knew of any… natural means from plants or herbs that Dawn Dee might have told you about to help strengthen the blood and give a person more energy?"

Mercy tilted her head and looked up in thought. "Hmm. I remember some things, let me dig out ma's journals and see if she lists anything that will help."

"Thank you." Jacob glanced around the churchyard for Charley. "I figure if we work from every angle, we just might find a cure for her.”

“Yes.” Mercy eyed Jacob suspiciously. “I’m sure your interest in helping Charity is purely for the good of the community.” She patted his shoulder. “Don’t underestimate the Indian remedies, though. Between Ma and Evelyn Graham’s knowledge of herbs, I’ve seen some pretty amazing things happen when it was thought there was no chance of relief.”

Jacob smiled. “No, I’m not underestimating anything. In fact, I’m counting on it.”

He spotted Charley. “Um, excuse me.” He dashed across the yard to catch up with her before she went back to the ranch. “Charley!”

She turned from helping her momma into their buggy.

“Can I come see you later today?”

“What about? Abigail?”

Jacob dipped his head. “You know I’m not interested in Abigail Drucker. Please, Charley?”

She glanced at her momma. “I suppose it would be alright.”

“Great. I’ll see you later, then.” He kissed her cheek, then stood back and watched them pull away.

Turning from the retreating buggy, he looked for his mother. She stood in the churchyard, again surrounded with well-wishers and curiosity seekers.

"Momma. Can we talk?"

"Yes, son."

He took her arm and walked with her and Poppa Monty toward home. "Would it be terrible of me to want to find a cure for Charity so Charley would be free to be with me?"

Honor cocked her head back from him and furrowed her brow. "No. Helping a person to be well, even with ulterior motives, is still a good thing."

He nodded. "I think Charity has some sort of weakness to her blood, like anemia. But her symptoms don't quite match what I've read about the disease."

"True." Honor smiled. "What do you have in mind?"

"Well," Jacob frowned. "I'm going by my gut feelings, here, but what if she ate foods rich in iron like liver and cooked it in a cast iron skillet rather than baking it in pottery, really induce the meat with the mineral. Is that crazy?"

Honor stopped to face her son. "No, son. That actually makes sense. Hmm. I never thought of that but it really makes sense. No harm in trying anyway."

Jacob nodded. "And I've asked Mercy to look through Dawn Dee's journals for plants that might help, too. I can't imagine Cousin Charity eating nothing but liver for every meal, but if she had it, say, three times a week."

"Excellent. There's nothing wrong with seeking help from Mother Earth." Honor searched her son's face. "You are such a natural healer, son. We've got to find a way to get you into Harvard."

"Well, I don't know about all that, but I know it's what I really want to do."

"I know, son." She smiled.

"Thank you, Momma. I'm going to go see what Mercy may have found and then I'm going out to Second Chance, I'll see you tonight."

"All right, son. See you tonight." She kissed his cheek and took Poppa Monty's arm. Together they walked toward their house.

Jacob hurried down to the livery. He didn't know if Mercy would look into her mother's journals right away or prepare dinner first, but either way, he wanted to talk more to her about this idea.

Jacob tapped on the Coffey Livery house door to find Mercy frantically sorting through bowls and pottery crocks. "What's all this?" Jacob looked around. Every surface and table was covered in dishes. It looked like the long tables at the Founder's Day dinner.

Mercy huffed. "Out of the goodness of everyone's heart, they have brought their untouched side dishes from yesterday's celebration that didn't happen because of Seth's incident, and brought them to me because my sister is at the clinic and not in her home." She looked exasperated. "Please say you'll stay for dinner."

Jacob chuckled. "Sure."

"Oh good. And after we eat, I'll get Ma's journals out for you."

"That's a deal." Jacob helped sort through the food and plated some selections to be warmed in the stove.

Adam, Mercy, and Jacob, along with Luke, Olivia, Cole, and Scarlett sat down and prayed before eating from the bounty that had been given to them.

Adam grinned at Jacob. "So, Abigail Drucker?"

Jacob frowned. "She brought Momma's food from Founder's Day and just stayed. We had no way of getting rid of her. Don't be making things up about her and me just 'cause you saw her sitting with me at church. It wasn't my idea, trust me."

Adam laughed. "All right, little brother. But watch out, when a woman gets her claws into a man, you never know what the outcome might be."

"You know Charlene Chance and I are destined to be together, not Abigail. We've just… gotta get some things sorted out first." He glanced at Mercy who smiled.

Jacob wished he had Dawn Dee's journal to peruse while he ate, but knew that would be rude. His momma never allowed him to read at the dinner table, despite the many times he had tried. Forcing himself to be patient, he cleaned his plate and took it to the washboard. Mercy disappeared and then came to the parlor with an arm full of journals. "Here. Help me look through these. Ma faithfully recorded her life and the things her ma taught her. Hopefully we can find something in these to help Cousin Charity."

They sat down and began turning pages.

Chapter Five

Charley and Hezekiah put together a meal from Saturday's leftovers. The family sat down together at the dinner table and bowed their heads. Hezekiah said grace and they ate. Charity picked at her food. "Charlene. I want to say something, and I really want you to listen to me."

"What is it mom?" Charley looked at her with concern.

"Why haven't you married Jacob Featherstone?"

"Mom!" Charley nearly choked on her food. "You know why! He wants to be a doctor and will have to leave Lantern to do it. I-I can't leave. I don't want to leave. You need me and—"

"Don't be foolish, girl!" Charity put down her fork. "You and Jacob have been together since you were small children. I know he's asked you many times to marry him. You're nigh on spinster age, what's holding you back. Don't you love him?"

Charley gulped. "Of course I love him. I've loved Jacob for as long as I can remember. That's why I tell him no."

Charity frowned and wrinkled her brow.

"He has dreams, Mom. Big dreams. I-I can't be

the reason he doesn't fulfill them. He needs to marry someone… like Abigail Drucker who's free-spirited and willing to move anywhere."

"Pshaw!" Charity hissed. "Jacob and Abigail Drucker belong together like oil and water! Girl, what is your problem? Didn't I raise you better than that? What are you afraid of?"

"I—" Charley looked to Hezekiah for help making Mom understand. He dipped his head and ate like his life depended on this meal. She turned back to her mother. "Mom, I'm not afraid. Well, maybe I am. I'm afraid if I marry Jacob and he takes me off to some strange town while he goes to university, and you get sick, really sick, I won't be able to come home and take care of you."

"Nonsense! Girl, you can't live your life waiting for me to die!"

Charley gasped. "Don't even say that, Mom. I'm not waiting for you to die! In fact, Jacob and I have been talking about finding something that'll help you get better. He's coming over later today and we're gonna—"

Hezekiah cleared his throat. "Charity, don't be so hard on the girl. Perhaps she has other reasons for not marrying the Featherstone boy."

"He's hardly a boy!" Charley said before she thought. "I'm sorry. I just mean he's twenty-four years old. Life has placed us where we just couldn't jump into marriage when we turned eighteen like so many others. We—"

Her words failed her. Why had she refused Jacob's every attempt to take her hand in marriage? She truly loved him and had no doubt he loved her. What *was* she afraid of?

"Honey," Charity continued. "All I'm saying is don't let *me* be the reason you don't seek happiness. You deserve to marry and have children and be happy!"

"Mom, I don't have to marry to be happy."

"Maybe not, but you *do* have to marry in order to have children! And frankly, I want grandchildren!" Charity laughed. "It's time this ranch had new little ones running all over it."

"See!" Charley sat up straighter. "If I marry Jacob, I cannot guarantee we would be here at this ranch for my children to run around, like you dream. Once Jacob becomes a doctor, he may want to stay in Boston or move farther out west. I have no idea what he'll want."

"Then ask him, dear." Charity's face sobered.

"Communication is paramount in a marriage, right Hezekiah?"

Hezekiah looked up startled. "Uh. Right."

Charley sighed. Was it really that simple? Jacob talked about going to Harvard and coming back to Lantern to practice medicine with his mother. But how could he know that was what he'd end up doing? And if he wanted to move to Timbuktu, but came back to Lantern because he knew that was what she wanted, then he'd resent her. That couldn't possibly be good for a happy marriage.

Charity leaned on her elbows. "Hezekiah, I believe I'd like to go lie down. Could you help me upstairs?"

"Yes, sweet one." He pulled his napkin from his lap and stood. "Would you like some tea?"

"No. I think I just want to rest a bit."

"Your wish is my command." He took her hand and arm and walked with her.

Charley stared at her plate of untouched food. What if her mother only had a little while left on this earth and she moved to Boston with Jacob and missed what little time Mom had? Would she be able to forgive herself?

She sighed more heavily. How she wished her

real father were here to tell her what to do. She cleared the table and put their dishes in the washtub. Set some water on to boil and shaved the cake of soap into the tub. While she waited, she took the leftovers from yesterday down into the root cellar where it was cool.

Alone in the cellar, she collapsed onto the steps, put her head on her knees, and cried. What she wanted and what she should do were so elusive to her. Why was it so hard to know what was best, or right? The gurgling water indicated it was boiling. She stood, wiped her eyes, and walked up to the kitchen to wash the dishes.

She might not be able to figure out what to do about marrying Jacob or staying in Lantern, but she could get the dishes washed and put away. That she could do and so she did just that and then went outside to see if Andre needed any help. Staying busy kept her from crying.

Jacob took Doc Holliday and a big saddlebag out into the open plains looking for the plant Mercy's late mother wrote about in her journal. "Good for the blood," she had written. It looked like a loose-leaf cabbage plant. Chickens and cows loved consuming it and so he had to ride beyond any homesteads or pastures. Finally, locating a meadow full of it along the river, he jumped down and began cutting the bowl-heads and putting them in the bag. Once harvested, he and Charley could cook and preserve it in mason jars for Charity to eat later. If it was anything like cabbage, he knew it would take a lot to put up a little, so he gathered as much as he could stuff in his saddlebag.

Jacob mounted Doc Holliday and rode along the river toward town. Huge cottonwood trees shaded his path and made for a pleasant ride. Suddenly, Jacob found himself flat on his back in the dirt, his breath knocked out of him, and Doc Holliday running ahead as if something had spooked him. Someone had dropped out of a tree, knocking him from his horse.

Jacob blinked and tried to sit up, but a boot shoved him back down. "We need to talk, Featherstone!"

The sun shone brightly, washing out the face of whoever held him down with his boot on Jacob's chest.

Jacob lifted his hand, trying to block the sun, so

he could see who this was. "What? Who are you?"

"I'm the man who's gonna stop you from marrying Abigail Drucker. That's who I am!"

Jacob swallowed, struggling to regain his breath. "Jaxon Ledbetter?"

"Yeah, Featherstone. Just 'cause your brother's been courting my sister, don't give you no right to take my girl!"

"What-what are you talking about?" Jacob tried again to sit up. Jaxon let him this time.

"Abigail's gonna be my gal! I been planning this for months. I'm gonna ask her pa's permission and then I'm gonna ask her to marry me."

Jacob shook his head. "Does she know this? 'Cause I haven't said nothing to her about courting or marriage or nothing. She's been the one to—" He needed to tread lightly. If Jaxon was infatuated with Abigail, Jacob didn't want to make her out to be as aggressive as she had been toward him, even though it was true. "I didn't know you were interested in Abigail. I'm sorry. Now I know, and I'll back off. I promise."

Jaxon staggered back. "You mean it?"

"Yeah, sure." Jacob crawled to his feet and brushed dirt off himself. "I didn't know you were sweet on her."

"Well, I am." Jaxon grinned.

Jacob looked for Doc Holliday. He grazed on grass under the cottonwoods. Jacob whistled and Doc Holliday lifted his head, still chewing, then meandered back to Jacob. "Listen, I've gotta take these plants to Charlene Chance out at Second Chance. I swear to ya, I won't make any more advances on Abigail, but do me a favor."

"What's that?"

"Go talk to her Pa and then to her today, will ya? Let's get this cleared up right away, all right?"

"You think so, really? I should just go straight to her Pa and ask him, today?"

"Yes. I'm certain of it." Jacob rubbed his sore chest. "Go now, Jaxon, and good luck."

"Thanks, man." Jaxon looked elated. He jumped on his horse that he'd tied down the river a ways and took off toward town.

Well, that solved one problem Jacob had. Now to go see if these greens helped solve another.

Chapter Six

Jacob chuckled to himself all the way to Second Chance Ranch. He had no idea Jaxon Ledbetter was sweet on Abigail. Thank goodness! This helped Jacob resolve the issue with Abigail without him doing anything hurtful to her. Jaxon had been right about another thing. Benjamin was seriously sweet on Jaxon's little sister, Jewell. Which was unexpected. As those two grew up, they seemed destine to be mortal enemies rather than lovers. But here lately, Jacob had seen a different spark in Benjamin's eye when Jewell came around. Could the winds be changing for his baby brother?

Jacob dismounted near the barn at Second Chance and pulled the saddlebag onto his shoulder. He had enough greens to cook a big batch to see if it helped Charity. Andre Hernandez waved to Jacob from the pasture. He must have been checking fences. Jacob left Doc Holliday near the water trough and strode to the ranch house. Charley came through the door, on her way outside.

"Oh, Jacob. I didn't realize you were here. I was just on my way to weed the garden."

"I've brought something for your momma, and a

couple of ideas I've talked over with my momma."

"Really," She eyed his saddlebag. "Let's go in and talk about it."

Jacob followed her in, slung the saddlebag down and dumped the greens on the washboard. "We need to cut away the stems and massage the leaves, then cut it into strips and cook it down. Dawn Dee wrote that it'll help strengthen your momma's blood. And I want to suggest she eat liver, fried up in butter in a cast iron skillet, no other way, three times a week."

Charley looked at him curiously. "You think these things will help Mom?"

"Yes, I do. I'm not positive, mind you, I can't find anything about it in the textbooks, but I've got a good feeling about it. I think your momma's got a special type of anemia. Those plants are rich in iron and the skillet will leach more into the meat. All we can do is try and see how Charity feels. It certainly can't hurt."

"No, I don't suppose it could hurt. Heaven knows we got plenty of beef liver around here."

"That's right. And I know where to find more of these greens. We can harvest some and preserve it."

"Let's get to it." Charley walked out to the spring house to get a beef liver from Friday's slaughter. She sliced it up while Jacob trimmed the greens and prepared them in a large pot with salt pork and vinegar.

He stayed through dinner and afterward he and Charley walked in the moonlight. Charley let him hold her hand. "Thank you for going to all this trouble for Mom."

"You're welcome." Jacob considered his guilt. "I'm doing this because I care, but—"

"I know." Charley turned to face him. "You're doing it so I can be free to marry you and we can go to Boston for you to attend university."

"Well, yes." Jacob confessed. "Is that such a bad thing?"

Charley smiled. He loved the way her nose crinkled when she smiled. "No. In fact, Mom practically chewed me out today for wanting to stay here to take care of her. She begged me not to let her get in my way of happiness." She dropped her eyes. A red blush filled her cheeks, making her even more adorable than she already was to Jacob. "I just can't imagine forgiving myself if I moved so far away and something happened to her… I just can't…"

Jacob took her hands into his and held them to his chest. "Charley, I know. Let's hope this dietary change makes a big difference, and your momma feels better soon. Then we can talk about moving to Boston. Besides, I don't know for sure that I can afford Harvard. I just want to know that if by some miracle all this works out, you'll be willing to go with me. And you know that means we get married before we take leave of here."

She looked into his eyes for a long time. "Please don't expect me to answer you right now. Let's see if Mom gets better. Then ask me again."

He smiled and squeezed her hands. "All right. One thing at a time. Besides, I'm really hoping to get a textbook I saw in the Harvard catalog and to help Seth with his recovery before I take off for several years. Waiting is not a bad thing."

She pursed her lips and closed her eyes.

Jacob couldn't help himself; he leaned into her and brushed his lips against hers. She kissed him back.

He lifted his head and gazed into her soft eyes. "Sealed with a kiss."

She smiled. "Yes."

Every three days, Jacob harvested more of the

greens by the river and took them to Charley. Seth came home and Faith notified Jacob his textbook was in. He read through it in a day and sought his brother to give him the good news. With the right kind of exercise and Jacob's help, Seth could strengthen his leg muscles and possibly stand. If he could stand, then he could possibly walk. Jacob was determined to give it a try. He quickly fell into a routine of harvesting greens for Charley and working with Seth in his bedroom.

Adam and Mercy married, and Seth surprised everyone with his accomplishment of standing. Jacob grinned from ear to ear when he stood behind Seth, in case he needed help, while Seth stood for the family. It was a beautiful thing to watch and reinforced in Jacob's heart that he wanted to do this for more people.

A letter came from Harvard. He was accepted into the Medical program. Yes! He couldn't wait to tell his momma and Poppa Monty, and yet… as fast as his heart soared with excitement, it dove into despair. Going to Harvard would be expensive and he could not imagine moving to Boston, working for someone so he had an income, and studying late into the night.

There was the possibility of another way. He had written to the university about it. It was a long shot, but only a matter of time to find out if he would be chosen. Then there was Charley. If these dietary changes helped Charity to feel better, then Charley would accept his proposal for marriage, and they could go together.

So many ifs and buts, Jacob wanted to yell out his frustrations! He stared out his bedroom window into the darkness and could think of nothing else but to pray.

Chapter Seven

"Oh, Jacob!" Abigail Drucker popped out of the general store just as Jacob rushed by. He crashed into her and grabbed her by the shoulders so she wouldn't fall from his momentum. "So… sorry, Abigail."

"I was just coming to give you a post." She panted, her eyes wide with excitement.

"Wha-why?" Jacob had been hurrying down the boardwalk to Seth's tanning shop. He was late because he had been absorbed in reading another textbook about the human musculoskeletal system. "I-I'm late for work. What post?"

Abigail twirled her hair around her finger, gazing longingly into his eyes. "I knew you'd wanna see this, it's from Harvard."

"Harvard! Really?" Jacob glanced at her other hand which held an envelope. She clung to it, not hurrying to hand it over to him. "Abigail, I-I can't… you… you're spoken for, right?" He released his grip on her, seeing that she was steady on her feet. "Jaxon Ledbetter, if I'm not mistaken?"

"Yes." Abigail twirled her hair and stepped back from Jacob. "Jaxon and me, we're getting married. I just saw this from Harvard and knew how important it'd be to you."

"Well," Jacob glanced at the envelope. "I thank you for bringing it—"

"Sure. There's nothing I wouldn't do for the Featherstones."

Jacob nodded, stepping back from her further, and waited.

"Oh." She giggled as if she'd forgotten the letter. "Here you go." She handed him the post. "I hope it's what you've been looking for."

Jacob stared at the envelope. "Yeah. I hope it is, too." He swallowed. "Uh, thank you." He rushed off to the tanner's shop. This could be the final word in the decision for him to go to university. If it was a yes, then he could go, but if it was a no…

Abigail was the last person he wanted to open the envelope in front of. In fact, he was in no hurry to open it at all, because it was so final if he wasn't chosen. He slid into Seth's shop and grabbed a leather apron, slipped it over his head, and tied it behind his back. He put the envelope into his pocket and set to work.

Seth still worked from a wheelchair and only stood when needed. The exercise was good for his strength building, but with the wheelchair at the ready, he didn't wear himself out completely, either. Jacob encouraged Seth to use his legs as often as possible and was beginning to notice his brother moving from side to side when he stood. Perhaps he didn't even realize he was doing it, but that was such a good thing to see. Someday, soon, Jacob knew Seth would actually walk. Jacob had asked Momma to order crutches before they started working on strengthening Seth's leg muscles. Now he thought it was time to order Seth a cane.

Benjamin had cut holes in the wood floor and dropped the vats and other equipment that was too high to work in from the chair. It sat on the dirt under the building and made it just right for Seth to process the hides. It was simple and ingenious. Benjamin had quite a knack for carpentry and reinventing things to accommodate a person's needs.

Jacob moved several hides to a rack where they could be washed and cleaned of the processing chemicals. Seth was in the back room, working on the ledger. Business had not suffered. In fact, it seemed to be doing better than before Seth's incident. Perhaps people were more attentive to bringing their business to him out of obligation for his hard work to recover from thwarting a bank robbery and basically saving those customers' funds from being stolen.

Seth certainly didn't see it that way. He continued to insist he did nothing to stop the robbers, but the town felt differently about it. Especially with him getting shot in the back. Jacob admired his brother's humility. Their real dad would be ever so proud of him. Poppa Monty was, too, of course, but Jacob liked to think Dad was in heaven watching over them and smiling. None of the sons of Honor had turned out to be less than he would have expected or hoped for.

Jonah strode in. "Hey, little brother, I was just on a lunch break. How you liking tanning hides?"

"Hey." Jacob smiled at his twin. "It's not bad. I get a chance to practice my surgical techniques and stitches?"

Jacob glanced at the back room where Seth remained engrossed in counting. "I got something from Harvard. Came in the post yesterday, I s'pose."

Jonah smiled. "Really? What's it say?"

"I don't know. Haven't opened it yet."

"Why not?"

"'Cause! I found out there's financial aid at

Harvard. An endowment of some sort. So I applied and I think this is their response. I figured it'd be a long shot, but why not try for it, right?"

"Right." Jonah looked Jacob over, as if he were looking for the letter. "So, why not open it and find out?"

Jacob took a long deep breath. "'Cause, right now going to Harvard is still a possibility. If I get accepted to receive this aid, I'll have the funds to attend. If I'm not chosen, then there goes my dream. It's all over, and I'll spend the rest of my life working here for Seth and wishing I could be a doctor… like Dad."

Jonah's eyes widened. "Jacob! You've gotta open that letter."

"I know." He hung his head. "I'm scared."

"I understand. Look, would it help if I opened it for you?"

Jacob lifted his eyes to meet Jonah. "I don't know. I guess. In a way, I kind of want Charley with me when I open it, and yet, if I didn't get the aid, I'd rather tell her later." Jacob spun away from Jonah. "I don't know what to do."

"Yes, you do."

Jacob spun back to face Jonah. They stared at

each other for a moment. Jacob swallowed and then nodded. "All right." He reached into his pocket and pulled out the envelope. He held it in front of himself and squeezed it tight between his fingers. Sweat moistened his palms. Drawing in one more deep breath, he peeled the end off and blew at the opening. The paper within rattled. Jonah rose to his tiptoes and peered into the envelope.

Jacob pulled the paper and unfolded it slowly. His eyes began to take in what the words said. His hand trembled and the paper shook.

Jonah cocked his head forward. "Well?"

Jacob read out loud, "We are pleased to inform you that you have been chosen to receive the Dr. Daniel B. Conant Endowment to aid students who attend Harvard Medical College."

Jacob squeezed the paper in his hand and fell into his brother's embrace. He whimpered against his shoulder. "I got it!"

Jonah sniffed back a tear. "I'm so proud of you, Jacob! You're going to Harvard!"

Jacob sniffed and stood tall. "Not yet. There's one more thing that's gotta work out."

"What?" Jonah glanced around. "What could possibly hold you back now?"

"Charity." Jacob uttered. "I talked to Momma, and Mercy has looked up natural remedies from Dawn Dee's journals. Charley and I have gathered some wild greens and she's cooking them for her momma as often as she'll eat them, plus beef liver. I'm hoping it'll strengthen her blood and help take away all this… fatigue she's been experiencing. If that has worked… then Charley will marry me and I can go to Harvard."

Jonah frowned. "You mean to tell me, after all this applying to Harvard and getting accepted, applying for financial aid and getting chosen, you'd still not go to university if Charley won't go with you?"

Jacob glared at his twin. "I love her, Jonah. I've loved her since we were kids. She promised me she'd marry me someday. We sealed it with a kiss." Jacob felt the heat of embarrassment fill his face. "I can't imagine being away from her for four or five years. She'd be thirty by the time I came back. I couldn't do that to her: Ask her to wait 'til I got back to get married. And I can't fathom letting go of her to marry someone else…So, yes. I'd give it all up and stay here if Charley won't marry me and come with me to Boston."

Jonah shook his head. "All right. I s'pose I understand. There's nothing I wouldn't do for Theodora either." Jonah looked deep into his twin's eyes. "When you gonna tell her you got the financial aid?"

Jacob looked at the crumpled letter in his sweaty hand. "Soon as I get off work, I reckon."

Jonah climbed on the wagon and turned to Jacob. "Well, good luck, then. I won't say a word to Momma or Poppa Monty. I'll let you give them all the good news when you get back tonight."

Jacob nodded. "Yeah, I hope that's what I'll have tonight— all good news."

Moths fluttered in Jacob's stomach all afternoon as he worked through his hours. He caught himself grinning from ear to ear, thinking about receiving the student aid, then he'd scowl thinking, if Charity isn't better, Charley won't come with him. Seth kept looking at him with curiosity, but Jacob wanted to talk to Charley before he told anybody else what was going on. Even his older brother.

Finally the clock struck closing time and Jacob cleaned up, hung his apron, and rushed out to tack his horse and ride to the Second Chance Ranch. Guilt swamped his heart again. He prayed as he rode. "Please, God, forgive me for my sin of selfishness. Let these foods help Charity and free Charley to be my bride and come with me to Boston. In Jesus's name, I pray. Amen."

Doc Holliday snorted and shook his head as they rode. Was he agreeing with Jacob's prayer? Jacob chuckled. "Good boy." He patted Doc Holliday's neck and urged him into a gallop.

Arriving at the Second Chance Ranch, Jacob slid from the saddle and let Andre take his horse, he ran to the door and beat on it.

Hezekiah opened the door with a frown. "Jacob, what brings you out this far?"

"I have something I need to discuss with Charley, Mister Brunston. Is she available?"

"Well, I… believe so. Please, come in."

Jacob yanked off his hat and followed Hezekiah into the parlor, where Charity sewed on a cloth stretched tight in a hoop, and Charley put down a book she was reading.

"Jacob!" She leapt to her feet. "What is it? Is everything alright?"

"Yes. I-I need to ask you something. Could we

step outside?"

She glanced at her parents and returned her gaze to him. "Yes, I think that'll be all right."

Walking at his side, they went out on the stoop and walked across the yard between the house and the barn. Horses whinnied in the barn and a goat bleated. "I come to ask you." Jacob stopped and took Charley's hands into his. "How is Charity doing these days?"

The moths that had fluttered all day in his stomach seemed to turn to lead pellets. He swallowed.

"She's… why? Did you hear something from Harvard?" Charley eyed him suspiciously.

Jacob threw his head back and sighed heavily. "I-might have, so I need to know, Charlene Chance…" He dropped to one knee, still holding her hands. "Will you marry me and come to Boston with me while I go to university? I promise, we'll come back to Lantern. I'll practice medicine right here in our hometown. You won't be gone more than four or five years. Please, Charley, please say you'll be my wife."

Charley stared at Jacob, her mouth hung open as if she were about to say something.

"Charlene!" Charity called from the stoop. Charley tore her eyes from Jacob's and looked up at her mother. "Yes ma'am."

Charity eased down the steps and walked slowly toward them. "Young lady, I told you! Do not let *me* get in *your* way of happiness! And I meant it. Now, Jacob is a fine young man. He wants to be a doctor, for heaven's sake. Who doesn't want their daughter to marry a doctor?" Charity made it to where they were standing. She breathed heavily. "I will not have you both giving up your dreams because of me! Now say yes, or say no, but say it because it's what *you* want! You hear me?"

"Yes ma'am." Charley frowned. "But mom, I —"

"Uh huh! No sir. You answer this boy's question truthfully! Or I'll take you to the woodshed myself."

Charley grinned. She turned back to Jacob. "The truth is, Mom *has* been feeling better since we changed what she's been eating. I mean, just look at her. She's come all the way out here all by herself."

Hezekiah stood at the door, watching with a huge grin on his face.

Charity had crossed her arms over her chest and taken a staunch stance.

Charley tilted her head. "So, now you be honest with me, did you hear something more from Harvard?"

Jacob ran his tongue across his dry lips, still on one knee. "Yes. I was chosen for student aid. I have the means to attend Harvard. But I'm not going without you, Charley. So, tell me, will you marry me?"

She sighed, glanced up at her mom and back to Jacob. "Yes."

"Woohoo!" Andre shouted from the barn.

Charley looked around and laughed. "Andre! Are you eavesdropping again?"

"Maybe, *señorita.*"

Charity took Charley in her arms and hugged her, then she hugged Jacob. "It's about time, you two. I was beginning to think this would never happen."

Jacob laughed with a lifted brow. "You and me both, Cousin Charity."

Hezekiah stepped out further on the stoop. "Let's celebrate. Come inside, Jacob, I've got a fine bottle of brandy I've been saving."

"Thank you, sir. But I need to get home and tell my family I'm going to Harvard… and getting married."

He cupped his hands on the side of Charley's face and kissed her cheek. "You wanna come with me to tell my family?"

Charley nodded vigorously. "Sure!" She wrapped her hands around the back of his head and pulled him toward her. Their lips pressed together and their passion unfurled. Charity cleared her throat. Jacob lifted his head and swallowed hard. Charley grinned mischievously.

Andre walked out of the barn with Charley's horse saddled and bridled. "I thought you might need your mare, *Señorita*."

"*Muchas Gracias*, Andre."

Jacob laughed and vaulted into Doc Holliday's saddle. urging him into a gallop. Charley was neck and neck by his side.

"YeeHoo! I'm gonna marry Charlene Chance!" He screamed as he rode down the road leaving Second Chance Ranch.

THE END

But, Reuben is next!

Personal Note From the Author

Dear Reader,

Did you know? The term "grownups" was first recorded as being used in 1805–15. Ha! I love research!

Alright, my friends. Reuben is the next Sons of Honor story. It won't be long.

About the Author

Lynn Donovan is an author, playwright, and director who spends her days chasing after her muses trying to get them to behave long enough to write their stories. The results are numerous novels, multi-author series, anthologies, dramatizations, and short stories.

Lynn is a co-host on a local AM radio show, KRLN 1400, called Write Time Radio where she and her co-host air old-time-radio dramas, narrations, excerpts and poems written by local writers, including herself.

Lynn enjoys reading and writing all kinds of fiction, paranormal, speculative, contemporary romance, and time travel. But you never know what her muses will come up with for a story, so you could see a novel under any given genre. All that can be said is keep your eyes open, because these muses are not sitting still for long!

Oops, there they go again...

You can learn more about Lynn on her blog at https://authorlynndonovan.wordpress.com, follow her on Twitter @MLynnDonovan, Facebook Author page at Books by Author Lynn Donovan at https://www.facebook.com/groups/BooksbyAuthorLynnDonovan and her website LynnDonovanAuthor.com.

Follow her on BookBub at www.bookbub.com/profile/lynn-donovan-9a8d7938-0798-44d7-b6e1-f52f55eb990d.

For more publications by Lynn Donovan go to:

Amazon.com/author/ldonovan

Newsletter and a Free Gift for You

Hey! Thank you for purchasing and reading my book, Jonah, Sons of Honor Series. I'd like to give you a parting gift to show my appreciation. Sign up for my newsletter here: https://lynndonovanauthor.com/newsletter. I will send you an e-copy of a collection of short stories I wrote purely for your entertainment. I will happily send you this e-copy for FREE, if you ask. I will also add you to my NEWSLETTER list and you will receive up-to-date information on new release before anyone else.

This book will **not** be sold anywhere, at any time, I am keeping it exclusively for you, my readers, and only if you ask for it.

Thank you again, and God Bless.

~Lynn Donovan

* 9 7 9 8 6 6 7 1 7 3 5 5 7 *